For Penny and Liam
—*M.W.*

For my great co-workers, Sue, Jane, Penny and Pam.
Thank you Alison for being a good model.
—*K.A.*

ISBN 0-590-45806-X

Text copyright © 1991 by Margaret Wild.
Illustrations copyright © 1991 by Kerry Argent.
All rights reserved. Published by Scholastic, Inc.,
730 Broadway, New York, NY 10003,
by arrangement with Omnibus Books,
part of the Ashton Scholastic Group.

12 11 10 9 8 7 6 5 4 3 2 1   12   4 5 6 7 8 9/9
Printed in the U.S.A.   08

THANK YOU, SANTA

Written by
Margaret Wild

Illustrated by Kerry Argent

SCHOLASTIC INC.
New York Toronto London Auckland Sydney

JANUARY

Dear Santa,

Thank you for all the presents, especially the knitting needles and balls of wool. They are just what I need because I'm sick in bed with a cold. But I'm not bored because I'm knitting lots of squares. My mom showed me how to cast on and how to do plain and purl stitches. Tomorrow I'm going to knit a square with different colors in it.

Love, Samantha

P.S. I hope you had a good Christmas, too!
P.P.S. Can you knit?
P.P.P.S. How are the reindeer?

FEBRUARY

Dear Samantha,

Thank you for your lovely letter. Hundreds of thousands of children write to me *before* Christmas, but I don't hear from many of them *after* Christmas.

I'm sorry to hear that you are not well. Our littlest reindeer is ill, too. He has a runny nose and a bad cough. Mrs. Claus and I are taking turns to keep him company all night.

Love, Santa

P.S. We had an excellent Christmas. A snowy owl visited us on Christmas Day!
P.P.S. No, I can't knit—my mom never taught me, and Mrs. Claus has forgotten how. Isn't that a pity?

MARCH

Dear Santa,

I hope the littlest reindeer is much, *much* better. I've sewn the squares into a jumper for him. Perhaps it will keep his chest warm. I hope it fits!

On Sunday we went to the zoo. I couldn't see a snowy owl anywhere. I said hello to the polar bear, but he just lay there with his eyes shut. I think he's very unhappy. Dad says our weather is too hot for polar bears.

When I got home I put on three jumpers and my hat and scarf and gloves, and I lay in the sun for an hour. Now I know what it must feel like to be a polar bear in Australia.

Love, Samantha

P.S. What do snowy owls look like?
P.P.S. What other animals are there in the North Pole?
P.P.P.S. Perhaps I should teach you how to knit!

APRIL

Dear Samantha,

The jumper fits perfectly! Here is a special thank you from the littlest reindeer.

He's quite all right now, thank goodness, but I don't think we'll let him pull the sleigh again next Christmas. He catches cold so easily. I haven't told him yet because I know he will be very disappointed.

There are lots of animals here in the North Pole. Mrs. Claus and I often watch them, and she does drawings of them. One of our favorites is the arctic fox. In winter its long, thick fur is pure white. It has furry feet and a bushy tail that keeps it warm at night.

Love, Santa

P.S. I almost forgot—snowy owls have white and brown feathers. The baby owls are white and fluffy.
P.P.S. How is your hot polar bear?
P.P.P.S. I would love to learn how to knit!

Dear Santa,

I loved hearing about the arctic fox. I wish I had a bushy tail to keep me warm in winter!

I visited the polar bear again today and he stared at me without making a sound. It's late autumn here so he's no longer so hot. But I'm sure he's worrying about next summer. I wish there was something I could do to keep him cool.

Love, Samantha

P.S. What do polar bears eat?
P.P.S. The littlest reindeer's going to feel very left out.
P.P.P.S. I'm busy writing a book for you. It'll be called *How to knit: Easy-peasy instructions for people who know nothing about knitting.*

JUNE

Dear Samantha,

Today we saw something wonderful—a polar bear taking her cubs out into the snow. They tumbled about and rolled roly-poly down the slopes. One of the cubs was very adventurous and went exploring on its own, but the other one kept close to the mother bear. Mrs. Claus did some terrific drawings of them. We pinned them up all over the house so now we have bears everywhere!

Love, Santa

P.S. Polar bears eat meat, usually seals. Sometimes a bear will wait for hours near a hole in the ice, hoping to catch a seal.

P.P.S. I know you're right about the littlest reindeer. He *will* feel left out. But he's still not strong, and we were very worried last time when he was so ill.

P.P.P.S. I'm looking forward one day to receiving your book on how to knit.

JULY

Dear Santa,

It's the middle of winter now and I'm hoping for snow. But mom says it hasn't snowed here in twenty years. So she helped me cut up paper into tiny pieces, then we emptied bucketfuls of paper over our heads and had our very own snowstorm in the living room.

Love, Samantha

P.S. Are there any birds in the North Pole apart from the snowy owl? Mom says in the South Pole there are emperor penguins. As soon as the mother penguin has laid the egg, she leaves it with the father penguin to look after. Because there is no nest, for two months the father penguin holds the egg balanced on his feet to keep it off the ice. Once the egg has hatched, the chick sits on the mother penguin's feet.

Dear Samantha,

The emperor penguin is an amazing bird, isn't it? Imagine balancing an egg on your feet for sixty days! Mrs. Claus and I tried balancing a ball on our feet, but we didn't last sixty seconds. I'm very glad I'm not a father penguin.

There are lots of birds here—puffins and terns and snow geese. The snow goose doesn't balance eggs, but it's still an incredible bird. Every September it flies almost 5,000 miles nonstop to a warmer climate, then in May it flies back to the North Pole again.

Love, Santa

P.S. Mrs. Claus and I are starting work on this Christmas's toys.
P.P.S. I still haven't told the littlest reindeer that he will have to stay home this Christmas.

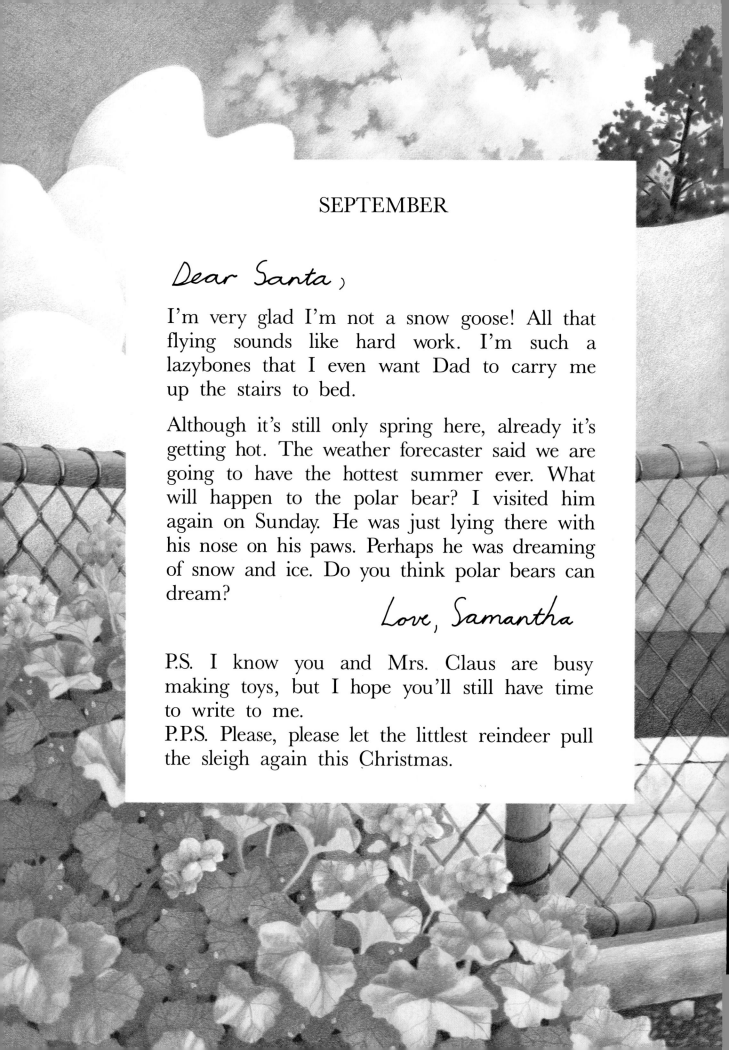

SEPTEMBER

Dear Santa,

I'm very glad I'm not a snow goose! All that flying sounds like hard work. I'm such a lazybones that I even want Dad to carry me up the stairs to bed.

Although it's still only spring here, already it's getting hot. The weather forecaster said we are going to have the hottest summer ever. What will happen to the polar bear? I visited him again on Sunday. He was just lying there with his nose on his paws. Perhaps he was dreaming of snow and ice. Do you think polar bears can dream?

Love, Samantha

P.S. I know you and Mrs. Claus are busy making toys, but I hope you'll still have time to write to me.

P.P.S. Please, please let the littlest reindeer pull the sleigh again this Christmas.

OCTOBER

Dear Samantha,

I told the littlest reindeer that he couldn't pull the sleigh this Christmas. I tried explaining that it's because we don't want him to catch another cold and get so sick again. But he doesn't understand. He thinks I don't want him because he's not as big and strong as the other reindeer. I wish I could think of a way to keep him warm during the long journey.

Love, Santa

P.S. I'll never be too busy to write to my favorite pen pal.

P.P.S. I'm sure polar bears do dream, especially if they are kept in a zoo. I'm not promising anything, but I will try to make your polar bear's summer a happier one.

Dear Santa,

This is a short letter—and here are some early Christmas presents. I hope Mrs. Claus likes the paintbox and you like the knitting book, wool, and needles. There's also a special present for the littlest reindeer. The scarf, woolly cap, and bootees will keep him as warm as toast, especially if he wears his jumper.

Love, Samantha

P.S. All I want for Christmas is for the littlest reindeer to be happy, and for the polar bear's dream to come true. Merry Christmas!

DECEMBER

Dear Samantha,

What a surprise! Thank you for the lovely presents. Mrs. Claus is delighted with the paintbox, and I'm going to start knitting soon. The littlest reindeer keeps jumping for joy. He will be the snuggest, warmest reindeer ever to pull the sleigh.

Love, Santa

P.S. Mrs. Claus and I hope you like the drawings of all the polar animals. Put them on your wall and it will be as if you were with us right in the middle of the North Pole.

P.P.S. Why don't you visit your polar bear on Christmas Day? We are bringing something special for him—something that will make his dream come true.

A merry, merry Christmas to you!

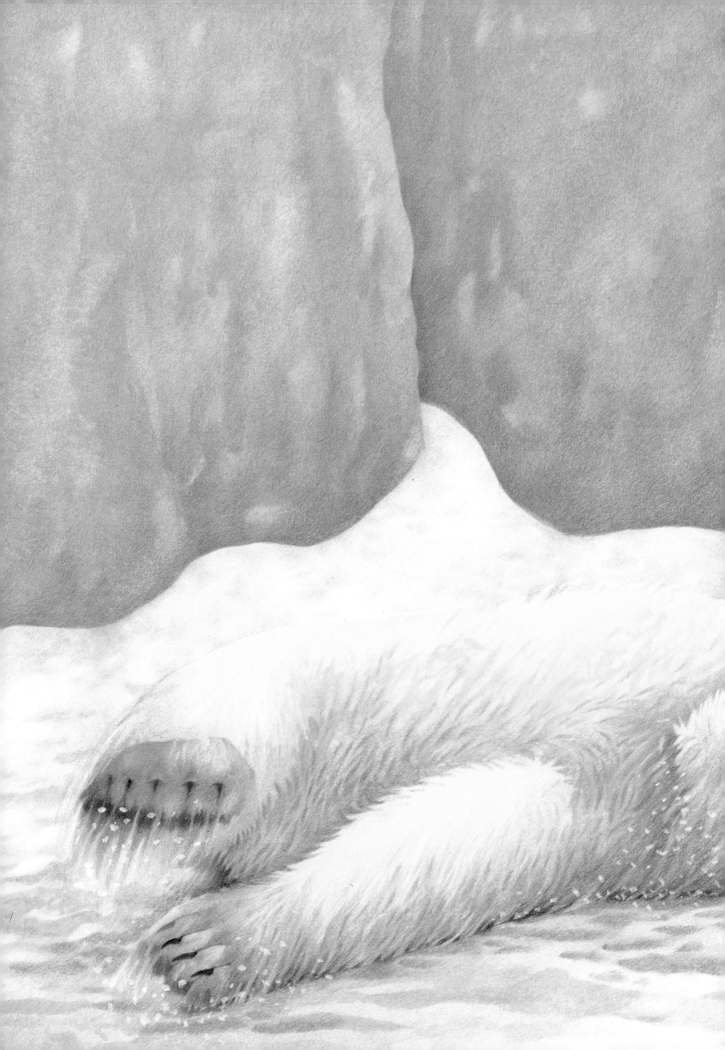

SEPTEMBER

Dear Santa,

I'm very glad I'm not a snow goose! All that flying sounds like hard work. I'm such a lazybones that I even want Dad to carry me up the stairs to bed.

Although it's still only spring here, already it's getting hot. The weather forecaster said we are going to have the hottest summer ever. What will happen to the polar bear? I visited him again on Sunday. He was just lying there with his nose on his paws. Perhaps he was dreaming of snow and ice. Do you think polar bears can dream?

Love, Samantha

P.S. I know you and Mrs. Claus are busy making toys, but I hope you'll still have time to write to me.

P.P.S. Please, please let the littlest reindeer pull the sleigh again this Christmas.

0-590-45806-X   Scholastic Inc.   RL3 005-008